Skeleton Cat

Skeleton Cat

By
Kristyn Crow

Illustrated by
Dan Krall

Scholastic Inc.
New York

Way down deep

'neath the graveyard mist,
where the groundhogs burrow
and the earthworms twist,
a skeleton cat began to wake . . .
and he climbed from the dirt
and gave his bones a shake.

He went: Rattle.   Yawn.

Rattle. Rattle. Clink.

Tip tap.

Purrrrrrrrrrrrrrrrr.

ka-plink,

ka-plink,

ka-plink.

Ghosts were a-moanin' and some bats zipped by,
and the skeleton cat said, "Where AM I?

I'm only BONES! How can this be?"
Then he leaped on the gravestones nervously.

He went:

Rattle, rattle. Clink, clink.

Rattle, rattle, clink.

Tip tap. Clickety-clack.

ka-plink,

ka-plink,

ka-plink.

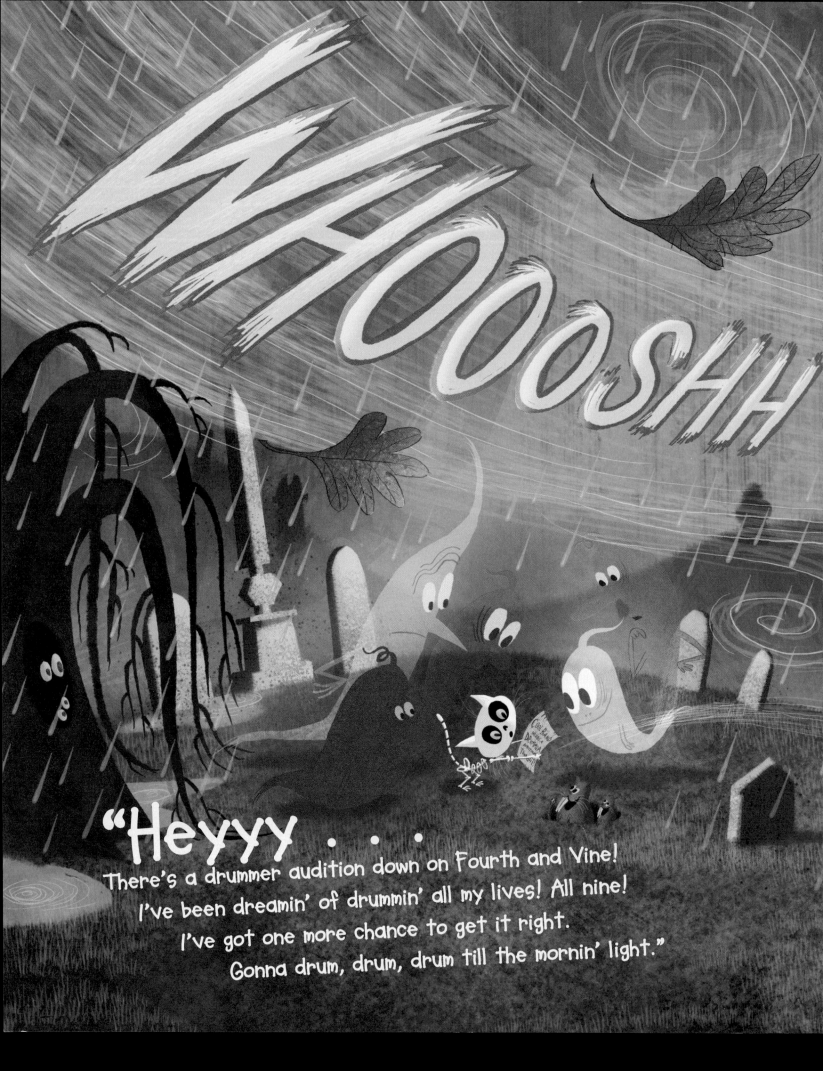

"Heyyy . . . .
There's a drummer audition down on Fourth and Vine!
I've been dreamin' of drummin' all my lives! All nine!
I've got one more chance to get it right.
Gonna drum, drum, drum till the mornin' light."

Well, the ghosts started laughin' and an owl said, "WHOooo?
In the living world? A cat like you?
You'll never be a drummer in a place like that!
You're a spook! A ghoul! A phantom cat!"

But the skeleton cat leaped through the gate,
sayin', "I'd better hurry so I won't be late!"

He went:
Rattle, rattle.
Clink, clink.

Rattle, rattle, clink.
Tip tap. Clickety-clack.

ka-plink,
ka-plink,
ka-plink.

He rocked and he rollicked
and he clunked around,

and the kids in a playground
heard the rattlin' sound.

SCHOO

"It's a SKELETON CAT!"
"He's CREEPY!"
"COOL!"

And they clapped to the rhythm
as he passed their school.

Then a dog tried
to race him,

and a cop tried
to mace him,

Well, he made lots of people in the city SCREAM!
But the skeleton cat still chased his dream.

He went:

Rattle, rattle.

Clink, clink.

Rattle, rattle, clink.

Tip tap. Clickety-clack.

Ka-plink,

ka-plink,

ka-plink.

He reached the audition
and he stood in line,
and they taped number 20
on his feline spine.

When the band members saw him, well, they called him nuts.
'Cause "You're not gonna make it
if you ain't got guts!"

So the band started playin' on that city street,
and the skeleton cat, he found the beat.

He went:
Rattle, rattle. Clink, clink.
Rattle, rattle, clink.
Tip tap. Clickety-clack.
Ka-plink,
ka-plink,
ka-plink.

"Sure, you've got rhythm, but have you got SOUL?"
So the skeleton cat went on a roll . . . .

BRRRRrrrrrrrrrrrrumble . . .
BRRRRrrrrrrrrrrrrumble . . .

Click clack ratta-ma-tat
clickety clackety plackety-plat
clunkety plunkety thunkety-thunk.
Tippity tappity clunkety-clunk
rudda-ma-tudda-ma-tudda-ma-tack
splunkety splinkety splackety-splack
clinkety clunkety
clinkety-clink.

ka-plink,

ka-plink,

ka-plink,

ka-plink.

Well, cats started watchin' from their windowsills,
and the real pretty kitties said he gave them chills.
So he passed the audition on that rockin' night.
Now he drums every evenin' and he's outta sight!

Rattle, rattle, clink, clink, CLANG!

ISBN 978-0-545-15385-0

10 9 8 7 6 5   15 16
                          40
Printed in U.S.A.
First edition, July 2012

The text was set in SoupBone Bold.
The display type was set in Bad Dog Regular.
The illustrations were done in digital media.
Art direction and book design by Marijka Kostiw

In loving memory of my
mother, Kathryn Gale Riley,
who taught me to chase
my dreams— K.C.

For Fuzzums— D.K.

Kristyn Crow loves cats but, sadly, is allergic to cat hair.
When her youngest daughter adopted a very fat cat living in their neighborhood,
Kristyn was inspired to dream up her own perfect hair-free cat, Skeleton Cat.
Kristyn is the author of many humorous books for kids, including *Bedtime
at the Swamp*, illustrated by Macky Pamintuan; *Cool Daddy Rat*, illustrated by
Mike Lester; and *The Middle-Child Blues*, illustrated by David Catrow.
She lives with her husband and their litter of seven kids in Utah. You can
visit her website at www.kristyncrow.com.

Dan Krall is an animator by day and a picture book illustrator
by night. His first book was *Being a Pig Is Nice: A Child's-Eye View of
Manners*, written by Sally Lloyd-Jones. He lives in California with his
wife and their daughter.